"Rachel!" said Zoe, breaking into a big smile. "What are you doing here?"

"I've brought someone," said Rachel, and she held the box out towards Zoe.

*With grateful thanks to Kate Steel (again!) –
guinea pig consultant, par excellence!*

ORCHARD BOOKS
96 Leonard Street, London EC2A 4XD
Orchard Books Australia
Unit 31/56 O'Riordan Street, Alexandria, NSW 2015
First published in Great Britain in 2002
A PAPERBACK ORIGINAL
Text © Ann Bryant 2002
Series conceived and created by Ann Bryant
Series consultant Anne Finnis
The right of Ann Bryant to be identified as the author
of this work has been asserted by her in accordance with the
Copyright, Designs and Patents Act, 1988.
A CIP catalogue record for this book is available
from the British Library.
ISBN 1 84121 794 8
3 5 7 9 10 8 6 4 2
Printed in Great Britain

Make Friends With
Rachel

Ann Bryant

ORCHARD BOOKS

Chapter One

Rachel was sitting at the kitchen table fiddling with her little red toy puppy on a chain. Her brother, Josh, was playing upstairs with his friend, Matt. Rachel wished *she'd* got a friend round to play, but they were all doing things with their families. Rachel's mum and dad had been gardening for ages. They'd just come in, both saying how tired they were. Her mum had started pottering round the kitchen and her dad had gone to watch a match on telly in the other room.

"Why don't you read a book, Rachel?" said her mum.

"I might," Rachel replied.

"Or make another of those collages for…"

But Rachel didn't hear another word her mum said, because she'd just spotted something incredible through the kitchen window. Her eyes flew open. It couldn't be…could it? It was all hunched up in a little ball, but it looked just like one.

"A guinea pig! Under our hedge?" whispered Rachel to herself, feeling a big buzz of excitement creeping over her.

Then she closed her eyes tight and opened them again, to check she hadn't just imagined it. No, it was still there. But it was hard to be sure that it was a guinea pig. It might just be a big clod of earth.

Her mum was running water into the sink so Rachel left the toy puppy on the table and crept out through the back door. She only took a couple of steps towards the hedge because she didn't want to frighten it away. But she was more sure than ever now. It *was* a guinea pig. What an amazing coincidence, because she'd only just seen a programme on telly, when a man had managed to rescue an escaped guinea pig. It would be so cool if Rachel could rescue this one. She took another careful step towards it. But the little creature scampered away. Just like that.

Rachel heaved a big sigh and kept her eyes glued to the bottom of the hedge to see if it would come back. By the shed was the empty box that her mum's plants had been in. That gave Rachel a brilliant idea. She would do what the man had done to try and get the guinea pig to come back. Bubbling with excitement, she nipped back into the house.

No one was in the kitchen. Good! This was Rachel's secret, and she didn't want to have to explain to anyone why she was taking two carrots outside. There was sure to be some grown-up reason why she wasn't allowed to catch the guinea pig. And if Josh found out what she was up to, it would be even worse. He'd be out here like a shot, trying to get the guinea pig for himself. Only he wouldn't have the patience to be quiet. He'd just try and grab it.

"Come on, little guinea pig!" whispered Rachel to the hedge. "I know you're here somewhere."

Rachel tore a piece off the top of one

of the sides of the box, so that when she turned the box upside down, there was a little hole like a low doorway for the guinea pig to go through. Then she put one of the carrots on the grass just outside the doorway. She snapped the other carrot in half and put one half just inside the box and the other half sticking out of the hole. Now the guinea pig would nip through the hole into the cosy dark hiding place to eat its carrot. This was what the man had done. It was such a neat plan.

But the tricky bit would come next. Rachel's heart began to beat loudly just thinking about it. The man on telly had hidden himself very close by and waited. Then when the guinea pig had gone inside to eat the carrot, he'd put his hand in the box and caught it. He'd been very careful not to crush the poor little thing, but he'd held on to it firmly to make sure it didn't escape again.

Rachel bit her lip. Perhaps she really ought to ask her mum to help. But as soon as she'd had that thought she shooed it away. Her mum would only say, *Don't be silly, Rachel. We've got nowhere to keep a guinea pig, have we?* But if Rachel had already *caught* the guinea pig, that would be different, wouldn't it? She crouched down behind the box and watched and waited.

"Come on, little guinea pig," she said, over and over again inside her head.

And on the tenth time of saying it, she nearly burst with excitement because it suddenly appeared!

Chapter Two

The guinea pig seemed to be looking straight at the box. Rachel didn't even blink. Just pretended she was a statue. The grass was beginning to feel damp under her knees. The dampness was coming through her jeans. But she didn't mind. It was worth it. And a few seconds later the guinea pig came out of the hedge and scampered along on its funny little legs straight towards the box.

It was hard not to gasp out loud.

Everything was working out just how it had happened in the television programme. Rachel wanted to jump up and shout out to her whole family that she'd done it. All on her own, she'd caught a real live guinea pig in her back garden.

But she knew she mustn't make a sound. From inside the box came a little scrabbly scratchy noise. Then a munching sound! Right. It was now or never. Rachel's heart was beating more loudly than ever. She didn't know if she was brave enough to do this. What if the guinea pig tried to bite her?

It was no good. She couldn't do it. She just didn't dare to put her hand through that little hole in the side of the box. It was too scary. There was only one thing she could do, but it might not work. She'd just have to see…

Quick as a flash, Rachel tossed the box away and grabbed the guinea pig with both hands. It wriggled like mad.

"It's all right," she whispered, as she brought it closer to her chest. She knew she was trying to calm herself down, as well as the guinea pig. It was trembling. Rachel stroked it gently and carried on talking to it. "Don't worry, you're quite safe," she said in a soft, soothing voice. "I'll look after you." Gradually it stopped trembling and nestled right into Rachel's neck. It felt lovely. Rachel thought she'd remember this moment for a very long time.

"I'm going to call you Snuggle," she whispered.

"Rachel! Who are you talking to? What have you got there?"

Rachel jumped up. The guinea pig didn't move. It seemed to be completely used to her now. Her mum was walking across the lawn.

"Look! I found it under the hedge. I remembered how the man in that programme rescued the guinea pig, and I just copied. It came to eat the carrot I put in the box, then I caught it! Isn't it lovely? I'm keeping it. I *am* allowed, aren't I? Don't say no, pleeeeease, because it's my best thing ever ever ever, and I love it. And I'll look after it and clean out its hutch and feed it and you'll never even know it's here, I'll take such good care of it..."

"Whoa!" said her mum. "What hutch? And anyway, this guinea pig belongs to someone, Rachel. You can't just take it and keep it. Some poor person somewhere is really upset because they've lost their pet. We're going to have to do a bit of phoning round and find out whose it is."

Rachel didn't know what to say. She'd been so excited, and now her body felt like a bottle of flat lemonade. She was too sad to speak. She'd never ever thought about it belonging to someone else. But she knew it was true. Unless...

"Are there such things as wild guinea pigs, Mum?"

"No. You've got to get all thoughts of keeping him out of your head, love."

There was a whooping noise, followed by loud laughing, then crashing out of the back door came Josh and Matt.

"Hey! Cool! Is it a rat?" asked Josh, his eyes lighting up.

"No, I wouldn't be cuddling a rat, would I?" said Rachel, giving her seven-year-old brother the look that she kept specially for him.

"We've got three of them at home," said Matt, sticking his finger up the spout of the watering can, because it wasn't as boring as looking at a guinea pig. Rachel was glad. She didn't want anyone else crowding round.

"Are we keeping it?" Josh asked their mum, as he rubbed the guinea pig's fuzzy fur.

"No, we're not," said their mum firmly. "It belongs to someone else."

"So ha ha to you!" said Josh to Rachel.

"Be quiet. It's nothing to do with you." Rachel turned to her mum. "We'll have to keep him till we find his owners though, won't we?"

Her mum looked thoughtful. "Hmm.

I suppose so, yes. I'll hold him and you nip next door to Barbara's and ask if we can scrounge a bit of her hay. I know she keeps a stock for the rabbit."

Rachel was about to ask if they could do it the other way round, and her mum go to Barbara's while she held on to Snuggle. But something told her that it would be a good idea to do exactly as her mum asked. Then she might get to keep Snuggle. And that would be the very best thing ever.

Chapter Three

The moment Rachel woke up the next day she remembered Snuggle. She ran downstairs to the utility room and scooped him up from his box. He began to make a funny high-pitched noise. Rachel had heard the guinea pig on the television programme, whistling. But Snuggle's whistle didn't sound at all the same. It was much chirpier.

"You're happy," Rachel whispered into his fur. "I can tell."

✿　✿　✿

At breakfast time all the conversation
was about what to do with Snuggle.

"Either we give him to Barbara next
door to go with her rabbit or we fix him
up with a hutch," said Rachel's dad. "I
know the box is big enough to keep him
safe, but he can't see out of it. And he
needs a water bottle and he's got to be
able to graze."

Rachel's body buzzed. It was brilliant
the way her dad was talking – almost as
though they were definitely going to
keep Snuggle.

Her mum was the problem. "And what
if I buy a hutch – and they're not cheap,
you know – and then his owner gets in
touch?"

"Well, I can't see that happening, to
be honest," said Rachel's dad. "I mean,

you've been round to all the neighbours and you've phoned the police. No...it looks like we're saddled with the little—"

"Don't you like guinea pigs, Dad?" interrupted Josh.

"As long as I don't have to have anything to do with it, I don't mind," said their dad.

"I'll do everything, I promise," said Rachel, sitting up straight.

"Don't get your hopes up," said their mum. "I've just had a thought. I'll ask Mrs Brown to make an announcement about it in assembly. You never know, it might belong to someone at school."

The buzz went out of Rachel's body.

"And if it doesn't, is Rachel allowed to keep it?" asked Josh.

"I suppose she'll have to," agreed their mum.

"That's not fair. *I* want one."

"Don't complicate things, Josh."

It was afternoon break. Rachel was playing horses with her friend, Emily, but she wasn't really having fun. She was holding on to the back of Emily's jumper, and trying to cling on while Emily went galloping round the playground.

"I'm going to invite you to my birthday tea," screeched Emily, as they tore round.

"Cool!" said Rachel. But she wasn't really concentrating. All she could think about was Snuggle.

Mrs Brown, Rachel's teacher, had asked in assembly that morning if anyone had lost a guinea pig over the weekend, but no hands had gone up.

It had been such a big relief, but then
Rachel started worrying in case it
belonged to someone who happened
to be away today.

Their mum came to collect Rachel and
Josh at the end of school.

"Is Snuggle all right?" asked Rachel
the moment she got in the car.

"See for yourself. He's in his box on
the floor there."

"Oh, you've brought him to pick us
up! That's so brilliant, Mum!"

Mum smiled. "Someone at work told
me about a lady who breeds guinea pigs.
I phoned up and explained a bit about
Snuggle, but I thought it would be a good
idea to go along and talk to her. I don't
know the first thing about guinea pigs. She
can tell us exactly how to look after him."

Rachel felt on top of the world. Her mum was talking as though they were definitely going to keep him now.

"Don't get your hopes up, Rachel. I'm not saying that we're keeping him. In fact, you never know, his owner might have got in touch with this lady to ask her if anyone's turned up with a runaway guinea pig."

Rachel's heart sank to somewhere below her knees. She didn't like the sound of this one little bit.

Chapter four

Mrs Elder, the guinea pig breeder, looked at Snuggle.

"Poor little thing, stuck in a box. Out you come." She gently took him out and held him against her chest. Snuggle started making his strange whistling noise. "That's a funny voice!" she laughed.

"Is that how guinea pigs talk? What's he saying?" asked Josh, wide-eyed.

Mrs Elder smiled. "I think he's saying

he wouldn't half like a hutch to live in!"

Rachel's mum looked anxious.

Remember we don't know that we're keeping him, yet."

"That's all right," said Mrs Elder, "you can borrow one of my old hutches for the time being. I can always provide you with a better one if you find that you *are* keeping him."

"That's very kind of you."

"Now, why don't I show you all my little guinea pigs?"

"Yeah! Wicked!" said Josh, as Mrs Elder led them to a big shed. "We could get another one. It could be mine, couldn't it, Mum?"

"Don't be silly, Josh," said their mum. "I can't be thinking about two guinea pigs when we don't even know if we're having *one*."

"Well, I don't want to seem pushy," said Mrs Elder. "But quite honestly, if you're having one, you might just as well have two. An extra one is no more trouble, and they do like to have a bit of company, you know. Guinea pigs get lonely on their own."

Rachel was feeling happier by the minute. She loved the way Mrs Elder was talking. It was beginning to sound like the most sensible thing in the world, to have *two* guinea pigs.

They looked inside twelve different hutches and saw lots of different types of guinea pig. There were brown ones, black ones, black and white, long-haired, short-haired, smooth, fuzzy. There was even one with a little tufty bit of hair sticking up on top of its head like a crown.

"Hey Mum!" said Josh. "Look at this dark brown one with the funny bit on top. Can I have him? I'll call him Spike."

Mrs Elder laughed. "Well at least you've chosen a boy." Then she turned to Rachel and Josh's mum. "If you do decide you'd like a bit of company for your guinea pig, I'd advise you to have a male. You don't want babies all over the place!"

Rachel liked the way Mrs Elder had called Snuggle "your guinea pig".

"I'm really not sure what to do…" said Rachel's mum, biting her lip. "I mean…would they fight or anything?"

"They might at first. But they should settle down after a while. If they keep fighting after the first day, just come back and swap him for another one."

"And what about looking after them?"

"Get the kids to clean out the hutch once a week and put in fresh hay. I can supply you with hay and food, but they mainly eat grass. The hutch is specially designed so they can go into the little house bit with the hay in it during the night, and go out and nibble the grass during the day. And there you are! Bob's your uncle."

Rachel was feeling so excited now.

"What about water?" asked their mum, still frowning.

"I'll give you a little water bottle to hook to the side of the wire mesh. Just make sure it's never empty."

Rachel and Josh stood there, perfectly still, looking up at their mum with pleading eyes.

"Pleeease," said Rachel softly.

"Pleeeease," repeated Josh in the same voice.

"Oh all right," sighed their mum.

"Yesss!"

Chapter Five

It was Emily's mum doing the school run at the end of school on Wednesday.

"Thank you very much," said Rachel, getting out of the car.

"Yes, thanks for the lift," said Josh.

Then the two of them raced straight round to the back garden. Both guinea pigs were nibbling grass but they bolted back into their little house at the sight of Rachel and Josh.

"I wonder if they've made friends yet,"

whispered Josh.

"I hope so," said Rachel in a worried voice, as she crossed her fingers.

Then, from inside the little house came a thump, a squeak and a big rustle of hay, followed by a whole series of squeaks and scrabbles.

"They're still fighting!" said Josh. "I hope mine's winning!"

Rachel's heart sank.

Their mum was just coming into the garden.

"Hello, you two," she smiled. Then she looked serious. "Are they still at it?"

Rachel nodded glumly.

"I've been watching them through the kitchen window and they haven't stopped ever since I've been home from work."

Rachel's heart beat faster. "I'm sure they'll be OK by tomorrow," she said.

"They should have settled down by now, love," said her mum. "It's been more than a day. I'm afraid it's not going to work."

Suddenly, out of the little house shot both guinea pigs. For a few seconds it looked as though Snuggle was boxing Spike, then he chased him back inside again.

"It's not mine fighting," said Josh. "It's Rachel's. Look!"

Rachel thought that Josh was right, but was afraid of what her mum might say next. "We could get another hutch, Mum."

"The whole point of getting another guinea pig was to give Snuggle some company," said her mum. "If we keep them in two different hutches they'll *both* be lonely."

"We could swap Snuggle for another one that doesn't fight," said Josh.

"No, he's *mine!*" said Rachel. "I'm not letting him go anywhere. He likes it here. Let's take Spike back and swap him for another one."

"But it's not his fault, it's Snuggle's."

"Well there's no point in standing here arguing about it," said their mum. "We'll give them one more day. And I mean it! Just till tomorrow."

Rachel sighed a big slow sigh. She really wanted to take Snuggle up to her room and play with him, but she thought she'd better leave him in the hutch with Spike to give them as much chance as possible of making friends with each other.

She kept an eye on the hutch all through the evening, but every time she looked, it was the same story. They'd come out of their little house and Snuggle would chase Spike round the grass, then Spike would cower in the corner and Snuggle would nibble at some grass. But the moment Spike tried to nibble grass next to Snuggle, Snuggle would nip him, then chase him round the grass again. And so it went on.

"Poor Spike," said Rachel's mum, coming over to the window. "If they carry on like this, I'm going to have to take one of them back, love."

Rachel shot round to face her mother. "Not Snuggle, pleeeeease!"

"Well, we'll have to see about that," said her mum. "Snuggle's the bossy one."

"But that's because he's not used to having another guinea pig with him." And just then Rachel happened to see through the window that Spike gave Snuggle a nip on the bottom and chased him into the house. "Look! You should have seen that, Mum! It was Spike biting that time, honestly!"

"Well, I've got the day off work tomorrow, so I'll keep an eye on them. If they go on fighting, maybe it would be best for me to simply take the pair of them back to Mrs Elder's."

"Oh Mum!"

"I don't know…perhaps we ought to think about females. Mrs Elder said they're not like males. They don't fight."

Then she went off to clear up near the sink, while Rachel stayed at the window, with a horrible sad feeling sitting like a brick in her stomach.

35

Chapter Six

All through school the next day Rachel worried that she was going to find an empty hutch when she got home. For once she wished she didn't have gym club after school. Now she was going to have to worry right up till half past five.

She told her friend Lucy all about it.

"Poor you," said Lucy. "But maybe a girl guinea pig will be just as nice once you get used to it."

"I know," said Rachel. "It's just that

Snuggle really loves me and he won't understand why he's not with me any more, if Mum takes him away."

"Maybe he's been good all day and he hasn't got to go after all," said Lucy.

"Maybe," said Rachel quietly.

It was Lucy's big sister, Kate, who took Rachel and Lucy home at the end of gym club. The moment Rachel got out of the car she hurtled round to the back garden. Then just before she got there, she stopped, because suddenly she couldn't bear to know what had happened. If Snuggle wasn't there it would be too awful.

After listening for a few seconds and hearing absolutely nothing at all, Rachel knew she had to go and find out. So, inch by inch, she crept forwards until she could see into the garden. A few seconds later she was near enough to see the hutch. The grassy bit was empty.

"They might be in their little house," she said to herself as she crept right up to the cage.

But there wasn't a sound. With trembling fingers, Rachel opened the door to the little house. It was empty.

Rachel hung her head as she went in to the kitchen. Her mum was bending down looking in the oven. She straightened up when she saw Rachel.

"Hello, love. I didn't hear you come in. I..." She stopped and looked at Rachel carefully. "What's the matter, love? Did something go wrong at gym club?"

Rachel shook her head. She couldn't believe that her mum didn't realise why she was upset. She could feel tears gathering behind her eyes.

"Look!" said a chirpy voice from the kitchen door.

Josh had come in. He was standing there, grinning from ear to ear, holding both guinea pigs against his chest.

Rachel gasped with happiness. Then she sprang across the kitchen and gently took Snuggle from Josh.

"Tricked you!" grinned Josh.

Snuggle made lots of little whirring noises as though he knew that he was back with his proper owner.

"He's telling you what a good boy he is," smiled Rachel's mum.

"Really?" said Rachel.

"He certainly is. He and Spike have turned into best mates!"

"Good boy," Rachel whispered into Snuggle's fur.

"And I've got some more good news...
Emily's mum just phoned, inviting you
to Emily's tea party on Saturday. It's
mainly family, but just one or two friends."

"Cool!" said Rachel.

Chapter Seven

On Saturday afternoon Rachel and Josh cleaned out the guinea pig hutch. They lined it with newspaper, then added lots of hay.

"I'll take the bag of old hay round to the dustbin," said Rachel, "while you go and fill up their water bottle."

"Then let's take them inside and start training them to do tricks," said Josh.

Rachel laughed. "You can train Spike while I'm at Emily's party," she said.

"But leave Snuggle in the hutch. You can't look after both of them on your own."

Rachel knew she didn't have to worry because her mum had already made that rule.

An hour later Rachel was washed and changed all ready for Emily's party. Her dad took her over there.

"Have a good time. Mum'll pick you up at the end."

"Happy Birthday," said Rachel, handing Emily her present, the moment she was in the hall.

"Thanks Rach," said Emily, her eyes lighting up as she ripped off the paper and caught sight of the squidgy yellow puppy on a chain. "That's really cool because my cousin Zoe got me a blue

one in the same collection. Come and
see it. It's in the kitchen."

They went through to the kitchen
and Emily sat the puppy on the kitchen
table, where it immediately started
barking a tune.

"Is your cousin here?" asked Rachel.

"Yeah, I've got all my cousins here
and two sets of aunties and uncles."
Then Emily poked her head out into
the hall and called out, "Zoe! Come
here a sec!"

"Oh good," said Emily's mum, coming
in at that moment. "Two helpers. Can
you take these through to the other
room. Take a tray each and go
carefully."

Rachel took the tray and set off at
such a speed that she nearly bumped into
a girl of about her own age who was

just coming into the kitchen.

"Sorry," she said, at exactly the same time as the other girl. Then the two bowls of crisps slid from one end of Rachel's tray to the other. That made both girls burst into giggles.

Rachel thought she'd never heard a funnier giggle than Zoe's. In fact it was so funny that even when Zoe had stopped giggling, Rachel carried on. And that made Zoe break into another giggling fit.

"I don't know why I'm laughing," she spluttered.

"Neither do I," said Rachel.

"Have you two met?" chuckled Emily's mum from over by the cooker. "You live quite close to each other, I think."

It was only then Rachel realised that

the girl was walking with the help of
a stick.

"Hi," said Zoe, in a suddenly shy
voice.

"Hi."

"Look at Rachel's present, Zo!" Emily
said, as she rushed off with her tray. "It's
on the table."

"Oh, he's so sweet," said Zoe, sitting
down at the table and stroking the
puppy.

"I'll just take this tray through. Back
in a minute," said Rachel.

In the other room, music was playing,
some younger children were dancing,
and all the grown-ups were talking
and laughing. Emily's dad was giving
out drinks, and Emily was offering
food round.

Rachel put the tray down on the table

and rushed back to the kitchen.

There were so many questions she wanted to ask Zoe, like: Why have you got that stick? Have you had an accident? Or have you got an illness? Will you be better soon?

But she didn't want to be rude, so instead she sat down with Zoe and asked: "Have you got any brothers or sisters?"

"One brother called Liam. He's seven. He's the noisy one in the other room!"

"I've got a seven-year-old brother too," smiled Rachel. Then she wrinkled up her nose. "He can be a real pain."

Zoe laughed. "So can Liam. He calls me Gertie Giggler. He got it from my dad." Zoe was still stroking the yellow puppy. "Do you collect these too, Rachel?"

"I've got the red one. I wish it was

real. I'd love to have a real puppy. I have got a real guinea pig, though. He's called Snuggle. Have *you* got any real pets?"

Zoe shook her head and for the first time Rachel saw a sad look take the place of her wide smile.

"I used to have a guinea pig," she said quietly. "I'd had him for nearly two years. But he escaped last weekend. I was just taking him out of the hutch – only I can't bend down properly because of my legs...I've got cerebral palsy, you see... And he nipped out and ran off...and I've never seen him since."

Rachel gulped. Her throat felt tight. "Wh...what did he look like?" she asked in a small voice.

"He's got really short brown hair, like me. In fact my dad says he sounds like me too. When he whistles it seems more like a giggle. So dad had this idea to name him after me. It's a bit silly, but he's called Giggles!"

Chapter Eight

Rachel felt as though the world had stopped for a moment. She couldn't speak. Her mouth didn't seem to be working. She just stared at the blue toy puppy that Zoe had given Emily, while her brain churned round and round trying to work out what she should say.

"Come on, you two," came Emily's mum's bright voice from the kitchen door. "We're going to play a game now, all right?"

"Great!" said Zoe, getting up and grabbing her stick. "You go on ahead, Rachel." She did a little giggle. "You'll be here all day if you wait for me."

So Rachel went, with a very heavy heart.

She couldn't enjoy the rest of the party even though it was really good fun. Nobody stared at her or told her she was acting strangely though, so she supposed she must have been joining in OK. But inside, she was miserable.

At seven o'clock her mum came to pick her up. Rachel said goodbye to everyone and thanked Emily's mum. Zoe gave her a special smile, and as she went out with her mum, Rachel heard her say to Emily, "I really like your friend. She's nice and kind."

"You're very quiet, love," said

Rachel's mum.

Rachel didn't answer. She couldn't explain how she felt and she didn't want to talk about Snuggle – or Giggles. Her mum would never understand how she was feeling. It was easier just to keep quiet and say nothing. Ever.

As soon as she got home, Rachel took Snuggle out of his hutch and cuddled him. He made his usual little whirring noise but Rachel couldn't speak, because it reminded her so much of one of Zoe's giggles. A tear fell on his ear. He twitched.

"Come and see what Spike's learnt to do," said Josh, appearing at that moment.

Rachel wiped her eyes and followed Josh into his room. She watched as he put Spike inside his slipper which was by the bed, then went over to the door.

"Come on, Spikey!" called Josh in a sing-song voice. Spike didn't move. "Come on, Spikey!" And this time Spike got out of the slipper and darted across the room as fast as his little legs would carry him, then got into the other slipper, which was by the bookcase.

"That's really clever!" said Rachel.

Josh's eyes were bright. "I know. I'm thinking of changing his name to Brainychops!"

Rachel went back to her own room and sat on her bed for ages, just stroking Snuggle.

After a while her mum came up and said it was bedtime. Rachel didn't argue, she just went off to put Snuggle back in his hutch.

When she was in bed she curled up into a little ball and shut her eyes even though she didn't feel at all tired. It was better with her eyes closed. She could forget about Zoe more easily.

A moment later her eyes shot open, because she'd realised something. She couldn't walk round with her eyes closed forever, could she? And suddenly Rachel knew what she must do.

Chapter Nine

In the sitting room her mum and dad were watching television. They looked surprised to see Rachel standing there, shivering in her nightie. Then even more surprised with every word that she gabbled.

"I've found Snuggle's owner. She's called Zoe and she's Emily's cousin. She told me she lost him last weekend. She said what he looked like and everything. I didn't tell her I'd got him because I was too scared of not having him any more. But now I want to give him back because he's got the wrong name here. His real name's Giggles. And I've just got to give him to Zoe right now. I can't wait till morning. She might be bursting with sadness!"

Without a word, Rachel's mum got up from the settee and hugged Rachel tight. "I'll give Emily's mum a ring," she said a moment later in a gentle voice.

Rachel sat in the back of the car with Snuggle in a cardboard box on her lap. She couldn't wait to get to Zoe's house.

"It's only two minutes' drive," said her mum. "Down Bramble Lane."

"Does Zoe know we're bringing her guinea pig over?"

"No, her mum said she didn't want

to get her hopes up, in case it's the wrong guinea pig."

"I'm certain Snuggle belongs to Zoe," said Rachel.

"I'm sure you're right, love..."

After a few more minutes they pulled up outside a beautiful house.

"I think this must be the house," she said. "It looks lovely, doesn't it?"

There was a bright light on the corner of the house, and another one in the porch so you could see the blossom trailing down the walls. One of the windows was in an arch with diamond-shaped panes of glass. Rachel thought it was the most wonderful house she'd ever seen.

"Do you recognise your home?" she whispered to Snuggle, as she got out of the car carrying him in his box.

Zoe's mum – Emily's Auntie Helen from the party – answered the door. "Hello again," she smiled at Rachel and her mum. "Zoe's just..."

"Who is it?" said a voice from behind her.

Zoe's mum smiled and opened the door wider for Rachel and her mum to go in.

"Rachel!" said Zoe, breaking into a giggle. "What are *you* doing here?"

"I've brought someone," said Rachel carefully.

The two mothers watched in silence as Rachel held the box out for Zoe to look inside.

"Oh Giggles! I can't believe it! You're back! Oh brilliant! Oh Giggles! But how...? I mean where...? I mean why...? Can I hold him?"

Everyone laughed at her funny speech —
even Zoe herself. Even Giggles made his
funny whistling noise.

"Come into the sitting room," said
Zoe's mum.

Rachel carried the box through and
put it on the settee. Zoe and Rachel sat
on either side of it and Zoe took Giggles
out. She gently laid him in her lap.
Immediately he ran up her dressing
gown and sat on her shoulder, whistling
loudly in her ear.

"He's pleased to see you," said
Rachel's mum.

"And I'm pleased to see him," said
Zoe. Then she turned to Rachel. "But
how come *you've* got him?"

This was the bit Rachel hadn't been
looking forward to. She opened her
mouth to speak but Zoe's mum spoke first.

"Rachel decided not to mention that she thought she'd found Giggles when you talked about him at Emily's party, because she wanted to give you a lovely surprise!"

"Oh thank you, Rachel. It's the best surprise in the world. But where did you find him?"

"Under the hedge in my garden."

"Thank goodness you managed to catch him," said Zoe. "Otherwise a fox might have got him. That's what Mum said." Then she turned to Giggles. "And guess what, Giggles – you're going to be a dad in a few days, because Molly's pregnant."

Rachel wondered what Zoe was talking about.

"Molly is Zoe's brother's guinea pig," explained Zoe's mum.

"I've got a good idea," said Zoe. "Let's go and put Giggles back with Molly right now. Then you can see what she looks like. I bet she goes mad when she sees he's come home. She'll probably whistle her head off!"

Rachel laughed as she got up. "OK then."

"Hold on a sec, love," said her mum. "It's getting late. We ought to be on our way."

"Oh please, Mum," begged Rachel.

"Or, Rachel could come over to play tomorrow?" suggested Zoe's mum.

"Yes! Brilliant!" said Zoe.

Rachel grinned at Zoe and nodded.

"Any time after ten!" laughed Zoe's mum.

Rachel's mum smiled. "Lovely! We'll see you tomorrow." Then she turned to

Rachel, and a more serious look came over her face. "Do you want to say goodbye to…"

"Here you are," said Zoe, handing Snuggle to Rachel.

Rachel kissed his fur. "Bye," she said. She knew Zoe was watching her. She managed a smile and a bright voice. "Bye…Giggles."

Then she handed him back.

"Thank you," said Zoe, looking straight at Rachel. "And when Molly has her babies, you can have one of them, OK?"

Rachel gasped. "Brilliant!" she said. "I'm going to call it Snuggle!"

The moment she'd spoken she remembered that she'd already told Zoe she had a guinea pig called Snuggle. Now Zoe was going to know what had happened really. She went pink and looked at the carpet.

"Snuggle's a good name," said Zoe. "Kind of special."

Rachel tried to blink away her tears. "That's because it'll be a special baby guinea pig," she said softly.

And when she looked up she saw that Zoe was smiling away at her. So she smiled right back.

Zoe looked at Jazz, wide-eyed and open-mouthed. She couldn't keep quiet a moment longer. "I thought you didn't like me?" she said softly.

With grateful thanks to Barbara Evans,
Thelma Searle and Pauline Smythe

Make Friends With Zoe is endorsed by Scope,
the national disability organisation
whose focus is people with cerebral palsy

Cerebral Palsy Freephone Helpline: 0808 800 3333

E-mail address: cphelpline@scope.org.uk

Website address: www.scope.org.uk

Make Friends With

Zoe

Ann Bryant

ORCHARD BOOKS

Chapter One

Zoe couldn't wait to show her friend Rachel the six baby guinea pigs and their mother, Molly.

"They're in here," she said, leading Rachel to the wide shelf at the far end of the shed. Very carefully, she opened the door to the hutch. "Look!" she whispered. "Isn't Molly clever!"

Rachel gasped. "They're so sweet! They look like a pile of wriggly furry sausages, don't they?"

"Yes," said Zoe, breaking into a giggle. "And Molly looks like a fat black cushion."

"Ssh!" said Rachel, clapping her hand to her mouth to stop herself laughing, because Zoe's giggle was very infectious. "You might frighten them."

Three of the babies had the same long black hair as their mother. The other three had much shorter brown hair, like their father, Giggles. All six of them were making little whirring noises as they rolled about.

"Which one's your favourite?" asked Zoe.

Rachel couldn't decide. "Er...which one did you want me to have?"

Zoe hugged her friend. "Don't be silly! I just wanted you to have one of Molly's babies. You can choose whichever one

you want. And as soon as it's old enough to leave Molly, you can take it home with you."

"Really? Whichever one I want?"

"'Course!" said Zoe. Then she frowned. "I wish they were all going to good homes like yours."

Rachel studied the little squirming bodies. "Aren't you keeping the others?"

Zoe shook her head. "We're going to separate Molly and Giggles so they can't have any more babies. We'll probably keep one male to be company for Giggles and one female for Molly."

"Have you found owners for the other three?" asked Rachel.

That little twinge of anxiety that Zoe had been having a lot lately, came back.

"Not yet, but Mum says it'll be no problem because there are always people

around who want guinea pigs. Only..."
Zoe wasn't sure that she ought to say
what she was thinking. Rachel might
think she was silly.

"What?" asked Rachel, taking her eyes
off the guinea pigs for a second to look
at Zoe. "What's the matter?"

Zoe bit her lip. "I know it's stupid, but
I wish I could choose the new owners
myself," she said.

"But you can!" said Rachel. "Why
don't you ask all your friends at school
if they want one, for a start?"

"I have," said Zoe, "and they've all
either got pets already, or otherwise their
mums say they're not allowed."

"The Head could make an
announcement about it in assembly?"

"The trouble is...some of the boys are
quite rough...and also...there's this girl

called Jazz Rawsthorne. She's in the year above…and I don't really like her, because…I don't think she really likes me…and what if *she* said she wanted one?"

"How do you know she doesn't like you?" asked Rachel, frowning.

"Because if she passes me in the corridor at school, or somewhere like that, she always looks the other way."

Rachel wrinkled her nose. "She doesn't sound very nice." Then her eyes strayed back to the guinea pigs.

Zoe wished she hadn't said anything about Jazz. It sounded really stupid when you said it out loud. Rachel was stroking one of the guinea pigs with her little finger. It was the one with the shortest hair, so it was the most like its dad.

"Is that the one you want, Rach?"

Rachel nodded. "Is it a he or a she?"

"A he," said Zoe.

"Brill!" said Rachel.

And as Zoe looked at Rachel's shining eyes, a really cool thought popped into her head. "You know, Rach," she said slowly. "I *can* choose the owners myself! Let's go up to my room and I'll tell you my idea!"

Chapter Two

"I'm not going to do joined up," said Zoe, concentrating hard.

"No, do it all in caterpillars," agreed Rachel.

"You mean *capitals*," giggled Zoe.

"Don't laugh," said Rachel, trying to stop herself grinning. "You'll go wrong."

Then neither of the girls spoke until Zoe had finished writing.

"Right," said Zoe. "I'll hold up the piece of paper, and you pretend you're

walking past the newsagent's shop and you see it in the window, so you stop to read it."

Rachel did as she was told, reading out loud:

"BABY GUINEA PIGS NEED GOOD HOMES

IF YOU WOULD LIKE TO OWN A BABY GUINEA PIG, WRITE TO ME AT THIS ADDRESS, AND SAY WHY.

WILLOW HOUSE
BRAMBLE LANE
NEWLISSINGTON
BR19 4NT"

Zoe's eyes lit up. "Just think, I might get loads of letters!" Then she frowned. "All I've got to do now, is persuade Mum to take us into town and drop us off at the newsagent's where they have

all the notices in the window."

"Are you going to tell your mum your plan?"

Zoe shook her head. "She'd only say there was no need because she can ask around at the Centre, or something like that."

"Is that where your mum works?"

"She goes there to help sometimes. It's not like a proper job. She got interested because of my cerebral palsy."

Rachel nodded, but she was looking at the card Zoe had just written. Zoe felt pleased. It was lovely to have friends like Rachel.

"I've got to go into town, you two. If you play your cards right, you might get a bar of chocolate each!"

It was Zoe's mum, who had appeared at the bedroom door. Zoe couldn't believe

her ears. They were about to go into town and she hadn't even had to do any begging!

"OK, Mum, we're coming," said Zoe, grinning at Rachel.

"You look as though you're up to something, young lady!"

"No!" said Zoe, opening her eyes as wide as they'd go to look as innocent as possible.

Chapter Three

"It's very kind of your mum to sponsor Zoe for the walk next Saturday, Rachel," said Zoe's mum, on the way into town.

"That's OK," said Rachel. "Have you got many others sponsoring you, Zo?"

"Yeah, quite a few," said Zoe. "But not as many as India Hunter. She's got loads of uncles and aunties!"

"I must say, I think it's a brilliant idea having a sponsored walk to raise money

for the school," said Zoe's mum. "It's lovely that whole families will be walking round the reservoir."

Zoe's mum smiled at the two girls through the driving mirror. Then she pulled up in the car park. "Right, first stop, the newsagent's. There's a book I need to get for Mrs Dean at the Centre."

Zoe and Rachel nudged each other at exactly the same time, and Zoe couldn't help a little giggle escaping. But luckily her mum wasn't paying attention. So she didn't see the big thumbs up sign that Zoe and Rachel exchanged in the back.

"I'll make sure Mum stays out of the way while you go and give the shop assistant the notice to put in the window," whispered Zoe, handing the rather crumpled piece of paper to Rachel.

"Here's the money."

"What if it's not enough?" asked Rachel in a whisper.

"It better be, it's all the pocket money I've got," giggled Zoe.

"Ssh!" whispered Rachel. "Where *is* your mum?"

"Over there, looking at books. Go on. Quick, before she sees."

So Rachel made her way to the till and Zoe went across to the book section.

"What are you looking for, Mum?" she asked, deliberately blocking her mum's view of the counter.

Her mum was crouching down, her head tipped on one side, looking at the titles of books on the bottom shelf.

"A book about the Isle of Man that Mrs Dean wants, but I don't think they've got it here. Never mind." She

straightened up. "Let's go on to the chemist." She started looking round the shop. "Where's Rachel got to?"

Zoe's brain whizzed into action. She didn't want her mum to spot Rachel at this moment. She might go over to the counter to see what she was doing. Zoe pointed at any old book. "Ooh! What's that book?"

"What?" Her mum leant forwards to look more closely. "This one?" she asked, as she tapped a book all about Finland.

"Yes, what's the capital of Finland?" Zoe was just saying the first thing that came into her head.

Her mum was looking rather puzzled. "Helsinki. Why?"

It felt to Zoe as though she was digging round at the bottom of her brain to find the next thing to say. "We were

talking about Helstinki at school."

"It's not Hel*stinki*, love, it's Hel*sinki*."
Her mum took the book off the shelf and
began to slowly turn the pages. "Look,
there's a chapter here all about it, Zo."

"Oh yes..." Zoe looked round. She
could see Rachel coming over with a big
grin on her face.

"Did you do it?" she mouthed.

Rachel nodded.

Then they both had to spend ages
looking at the book about Finland with
Zoe's mum, and trying to keep straight
faces at the same time.

Chapter Four

Zoe was walking up the road to her keyboard lesson. Mrs Willets, her teacher, lived just a few houses away from Zoe's house.

"Oh, Mrs Willets said to take your sponsorship form along to your lesson," called Zoe's mum from their front gate.

"I've got it," said Zoe.

Then she gave her mum a final wave as she turned into Mrs Willets's drive.

This week Zoe's lesson was on a

different day from usual. She'd done a swap with another one of Mrs Willets's pupils who couldn't manage her regular time.

Mrs Willets liked her pupils to let themselves in at the back door. Then when it was time for their lesson they were supposed to creep into the music room quietly and wait until Mrs Willets had finished with the pupil before.

It was exactly quarter to five when Zoe was standing outside the music room. She'd started to feel anxious, because it was going to be a different pupil from usual in there. If they weren't actually playing the piano or keyboard at that moment, they might stare at Zoe when they saw her stick and the way she walked. She always hated that.

Through the door Zoe could hear that

this pupil was playing the keyboard. The piece sounded really good. Before she could change her mind, she tapped lightly on the door and pushed it open.

In the doorway she froze, because sitting at the keyboard was Jazz Rawsthorne.

Zoe's heart started banging against her ribcage, as she quickly put her stick in the same hand as her music bag, so she could push the door shut behind her with the other one. Jazz was busy concentrating on her music, while Mrs Willets pointed along the notes, counting to keep Jazz in time.

But Zoe knew that the moment she'd finished her piece Jazz would look round. Then, when she saw who was standing there, she'd snap her eyes straight back on her music again. What if Mrs Willets said, "Do you two know each other?"

and Jazz didn't answer? Mrs Willets would wonder what was wrong. She might think Zoe had done something to annoy Jazz. It would all be horrible and embarrassing.

If Zoe could just get behind Jazz before she finished playing through her piece, then Jazz wouldn't know who was there, unless she swivelled right round on the stool. But Zoe was flustered because she was trying to hurry, so she dropped her stick. It knocked against the door with a loud clack. Immediately, Jazz stopped playing and looked round. But the moment she saw Zoe she quickly fastened her eyes back on her music, just as Zoe had guessed she would.

"Hello Zoe!" said Mrs Willets in her usual sing-song voice. Then she jumped up and picked up the stick. "There you

are, love. I'll only be a minute or two. Do you two girls know each other?"

Zoe gulped.

"Yes," whispered Jazz, her eyes still firmly on her music.

Zoe only managed a nod. She could feel herself going red, and pretended to be very interested in something going on out of the window. Mrs Willets didn't seem to notice anything was the matter. She counted away as Jazz played the last bit of her piece.

As soon as the piece was finished, Mrs Willets started writing in Jazz's practice book, and talking to her at the same time. Then Jazz began to pack away her music. Her hair was falling over her face. Zoe wondered if she'd deliberately let it fall like that, to make sure there was absolutely no chance of having to

look at Zoe. Not even by mistake.

"Oh," said Jazz to Mrs Willets, pulling a sheet of paper out of her bag. "Mum wondered if you'd mind sponsoring me for the walk we're doing on Saturday?"

"Of course I will. I've heard all about this sponsored walk. I think it's a great idea!"

Mrs Willets signed Jazz's form, then she turned to Zoe. "Have you brought yours along, dear? I could be filling it in while you get your music out."

So Zoe got the form out of her bag, while Jazz put her form away and went to the door without looking in Zoe's direction even once.

"See you next week," warbled Mrs Willets.

"Bye," said Jazz. Then she rushed out of the room, her eyes on the carpet.

Zoe breathed a big sigh of relief. If Mrs Willets ever asked her to swap to this time again, she'd have to make up an excuse why she couldn't come.

"Right, let's see how your piece is coming along," said Mrs Willets brightly.

As soon as she started playing, Zoe forgot about everything except the music. She had composed the piece by working out exactly how the tune should sound, then deciding on the speed and the beat and what instruments she wanted. Zoe had done lots of practice on her piece since the last lesson, because she was going to be playing it in assembly the next day. As she played it for Mrs Willets, she had to concentrate hard on making sure she pressed the right buttons and the right keys at the right time.

The whole lesson was really good fun.

"I *am* impressed Zoe!" said Mrs Willets at the end. "You're such a musical girl, you know. That melody you've worked out is absolutely wonderful. I wish I could get some of my other keyboard pupils to compose like you do! Anyway, I think you're all ready for tomorrow now. I'm sure you'll bring the roof down! But I hope you don't, because it might cost quite a bit to fix it!"

Zoe giggled.

"Right, you can pack away, dear. My next pupil's away so I'm going to play the piano myself now. It's my treat. Can you let yourself out?"

Zoe nodded and Mrs Willets held the door open for her. "Bye, dear. I'll be thinking about you tomorrow at assembly time. And if the roof *does* come down, ask the head teacher to send

the bill to me, all right!"

Zoe was giggling as she met her mum in the hall.

"So it was a good lesson then, love?"

Zoe nodded thoughtfully. It had been a bit of a strange mixture lesson.

Chapter Five

The very moment Zoe opened her eyes the next morning a nervous feeling came over her. The feeling stayed with her all through breakfast and right till she got to school.

In the classroom, surrounded by friends, it went away a little bit.

"What are you playing, Zo?"

"Quite a complicated piece. I'm worried that I might forget what comes next halfway through."

"No you won't," said Olivia, giving Zoe a hug.

"'Course not. You're wicked at composing on the keyboard," said India. "Everybody will sit there gobsmacked, wishing they were as clever as you."

At nine o'clock the whole school filed into the hall in their class lines. You had to be completely silent in assembly. The head teacher, Mrs James, stood at the front. Next to her was the keyboard on a table. While the rest of Zoe's class sat down in two rows as usual, Zoe walked slowly up to the keyboard and sat down on the chair.

As she put her music on the stand she tried to remember what her mum had said to her on the way to school in the car, when Zoe had been worrying

about everyone looking at her.

"Of course they'll be looking at you, love," she had said. "They won't have anything else to watch, will they, sitting there in their rows? Just remember they're only interested in you because you've been chosen to play, so you must be special."

Once her music was in place, Zoe dared to look out at all the faces. Olivia and India were grinning and waving from halfway down the hall. Zoe gave them a shaky smile, but the smile faded away when she saw who was sitting two rows behind Olivia. It was Jazz. She was looking at Zoe and whispering to the girl next to her. But the second she saw Zoe looking, she stopped whispering and fixed her eyes on the floor.

"Right," said Mrs James, when

everybody was seated. "We've got a lovely treat this morning because Zoe is going to play for us." She smiled broadly at Zoe. "And I believe you made up the piece yourself, didn't you, Zoe?"

Zoe nodded and tried not to go pink.

"Would you like to announce the title then?"

Zoe gulped. She'd never given the piece a title. She quickly tried to think of something good. "Er...it's called...er..."

"What about *The Lake*?" someone called out.

Zoe's heart missed a beat. It was Jazz. She'd sounded normal, though. She hadn't spoken in a nasty voice. But Zoe was confused. How had Jazz known that the piece really *did* sound smooth and watery? For a second their eyes met, but as usual Jazz looked straight down, and

Zoe was left feeling flustered and more nervous than ever.

"*The Lake*," repeated Mrs James. "Is that all right, Zoe?"

Again Zoe nodded, feeling her face going red this time.

"Right, start when you're ready."

With trembling fingers, Zoe began to play her piece. She made a slip almost immediately, and that made her fingers tremble even more. But a few seconds later, when she hadn't made any more mistakes, she began to feel a little bit better. Then just over halfway through the piece, her fingers stopped trembling, and she forgot all about everything except the music she was making.

It gave her a shock when the clapping started. It was so loud. She kept her eyes on the keyboard at first, then

glanced across at Mrs James.

"Well done!" she mouthed, as she carried on clapping with everyone else.

So then Zoe decided she'd risk a quick glance at the rows of pupils. India was grinning like mad, and Olivia had got her thumbs up, only she was making them do a sort of dance in the air. Zoe couldn't help giggling, but she stopped immediately, because behind them, Jazz was clapping with her eyes on the ground.

As the clapping faded Mrs James walked across, handed Zoe her stick and whispered, "That was excellent, Zoe. Come and sit at the side here, dear."

Zoe took a few steps to the chair that Mrs James had put out for her, and sat down in it. At that moment, for the first time for a long time, Zoe felt angry

about her legs. If only she could have zipped straight back to Olivia's row, threaded her way along the crossed legs until she'd got to Olivia and plonked herself down right beside her. But zipping and threading and plonking were not things that Zoe would ever be able to do.

She sighed without letting it show, and stared at the floor.

Chapter Six

Two days later a letter arrived for Zoe.

"I wonder who it's from?" said her mum, handing it to Zoe, then going back to making breakfast.

Zoe opened it at the table. She felt so excited. Inside was a card with a picture of a guinea pig on the front, stuck over the real picture on the card. Zoe began to read to herself what it said on the inside of the card.

Hello,

I saw your sort of advert in the newsagents. My brother and I used to have two guinea pigs – one each. But Rory's one died. Rory is a bit older than me (I am nine) but he still cried. I felt really sorry for him and I want to buy him a new one with my pocket money. My mum says that's OK. How much do your guinea pigs cost?

Love from Jade

"Look!" cried Zoe, without thinking.

Her mum came over, smiling. "Who's it from, Zo?"

Zoe bit her lip. She'd been so excited about getting a letter that she'd completely forgotten that her mum didn't know anything about her advert.

"Er...it's a letter about the guinea pigs."

"A letter about the guinea pigs?

What do you mean?"

"Well…you know I was worrying about the baby guinea pigs?"

"Mmm," said her mum, pursing her lips and looking straight into Zoe's eyes. "Go on."

"Because I wanted to be sure they all went to good homes like Rachel's, you see…"

"Mmm…" Her mum was wearing the look that she usually wore if she was about to be cross. "So what have you been up to?"

Zoe spoke in a soft voice because it seemed less of a naughty thing to have done if she only said it quietly. "You know that day when we took Rachel into town… Well, I put an advertisement in the newsagent's window…or rather, I got Rachel to do it…"

Her mum frowned. "You really shouldn't have done that without asking, Zoe."

"Sorry."

"What did it say?"

"Only my address and that I'd got guinea pigs that needed good homes."

"Well, children shouldn't put adverts in shop windows without their parents' permission. Remember that in future, Zoe."

"Sorry," said Zoe again.

Then her mum wagged her finger, but it was obvious she wasn't so cross any more. "I knew something dodgy was going on in that newsagent's, you know! Helstinki indeed!"

Zoe let out a nervous giggle. "I only did it for the guinea pigs' sakes. You wouldn't like them to go to bad homes

and be miserable, would you?"

Her mum ignored that question and asked one of her own. "So someone's replied, have they?"

Zoe nodded. "She sounds really nice. She's called Jade. Here. You can read it."

Zoe's mum read the letter quickly. "Yes, you're right. She does sound nice. There's only one problem."

"What?"

"She's not put her phone number or her address or even her surname."

Zoe's face fell as she looked again at the letter and then searched all over the envelope for any sign of an address.

"How can we find out?" she finally asked her mum in a small voice.

"I'm afraid we can't, love. You'll just have to hope she suddenly realises and writes to you again." Zoe heaved a big

sigh. "But I shouldn't worry. It won't be a problem finding homes for baby guinea pigs. I'll ask at the Centre."

Zoe sighed. "OK." But it wasn't really OK. What if Jade didn't realise she hadn't put her surname or her address on the letter? She'd think Zoe had decided not to choose her, and she might be upset.

It was odd – Zoe had never even met Jade, and yet she was feeling sorry for her at this moment.

Chapter Seven

On Saturday afternoon at two o'clock, Zoe, her mum, her dad and her younger brother, Liam, piled out of their car into the reservoir car park. There were quite a few other cars there.

"Looks like the school is going to raise a fair amount of money," said Zoe's dad.

"Yes, it's great that it's so popular," said Zoe's mum.

The walk was probably going to take about an hour and a half. When twenty

minutes or so had gone by, Zoe's arm
and hand ached from gripping the stick
so hard, and her legs and feet were
beginning to ache too. Her mum had
offered to bring the buggy along in case
Zoe got tired, but Zoe had insisted that
she'd be fine.

"Are you all right, love?" said her
mum. "We can stop for a sit down on
this seat if you want?"

Zoe shook her head.

Just then they heard some pounding
footsteps and Olivia and India came
puffing up behind them.

"We've been trying to catch you up,"
said India.

"You must be slower than a snail if
you can't even catch *me* up," said Zoe,
breaking into a giggle.

"That's enough of that," smiled Zoe's

dad, as Olivia and India broke into giggles too.

"Oh there's Ruth from the Centre," said Zoe's mum. "Do you mind if Dad and I catch her up, Zo?"

"We'll walk with Zoe," said Olivia.

"I'll come with you two," said Liam. "I don't want to stay with a load of girls."

"Come on, then," said Zoe's mum, breaking into a jog. "Ruth seems to have put on a spurt!"

"Do you want a King's Carry, Zo?" asked Olivia.

"Won't I be too heavy?"

"No, it'll be easy," said India. "Come on!"

So, clutching her stick, Zoe put her arms round Olivia's and India's shoulders, while they held hands to

make the King's seat.

"This is luxury!" said Zoe, tipping her smiling face back to feel the warm sunshine.

"You feel light as a feather," said Olivia.

Zoe smiled. But then her lovely happy feelings dissolved because she clearly heard Jazz Rawsthorne's voice behind her.

"Is it OK if we go on ahead a bit with Tod, Auntie Barbara?"

"Yes of course," came the reply.

✿ ✿ ✿

Chapter Eight

Zoe suddenly felt stupid being carried along. "It's OK," she quickly told Olivia and India, "I'll walk now."

The girls put Zoe down and Jazz went past with a boy who looked just like her but a bit older, who must have been her brother, and a little boy with fair curly hair, who looked about four.

"I want a carry like that big girl," said the little boy, tugging at Jazz's sleeve.

Zoe heard Jazz say, "You can in a

minute, Tod. Let's have a run first, shall we?"

Then she got hold of one of Tod's hands and her brother got hold of the other, and the two of them scooped him up off the ground as they ran along.

Jazz thinks King's Carries are stupid, now she's seen me having one, Zoe said to herself, feeling even more upset.

Then she heard Jazz's brother say, "We'd better not go too far."

And one of their mothers must have had the same thought, because she called out, "Don't get too far ahead, you three!"

But Zoe didn't think Jazz and the boy could have heard because they kept running along and whizzing Tod up in the air, which made him giggle like mad.

"Look!" said Olivia, pointing, "They're going down the bank towards the water.

My mum said I definitely wasn't allowed to do that."

"So did mine," said India, "I bet their mums and dads will be mad when they find out they've gone down there."

"Their parents aren't even looking," said Olivia, turning to look behind. "They've stopped to talk to someone."

"Perhaps Jazz and the others are hiding from their parents on purpose," said Zoe, "and they're going to jump out on them when they go past."

But as they drew nearer they heard Tod's voice coming from somewhere down the bank. He was singing loudly.

"Row, row, row your boat,
Gently down the stream,
Merrily, merrily, merrily, merrily,
Life is but a dream."

"Be careful, Tod!" came Jazz's anxious voice. "Not too near the edge!"

"I'm OK," said Tod. "I'm rowing my boat. Look!"

"Let's see what he's doing," said India. "He sounds so sweet, doesn't he?"

Zoe didn't want to go where Jazz might spot her so she stood just behind the other two, but she could see Tod sitting right at the bottom of the bank. Jazz's brother was showing Jazz how to skim stones across the water.

"You've got to throw them sideways," he was saying. "Like this."

But Jazz was watching Tod. "Come away from the edge, Tod! You're too close."

Tod ignored her.

"Row, row, row your boat..."

He was pretending to row as he sang.

Then he suddenly looked up and saw Zoe and the others watching him. Immediately he broke into a big grin, and carried on with much bigger rows, as though he was in the Olympic Games.

"Merrily, merrily, merrily, mer—"

There was a splash as Tod toppled in. Zoe and the others gasped as he disappeared under the water. The next second, the fair curly head came bobbing up and Tod started splashing the water with his hands, but that only made him go further away from the bank. He started screaming his head off.

"Go and get help! Quick!" yelled Jazz's brother, looking terrified, as he crouched down. "I'll get him out!"

"Help!" cried Jazz, looking up at Zoe and the others. "Help, it's really deep!" But she didn't move at all. She seemed

frozen to the spot.

Zoe knew she had to think quickly. Her brain whizzed at a hundred miles per hour. Her parents were a long way ahead. And far behind, Jazz's and Tod's mums were still chatting to their friends.

"You run back to those grown-ups behind," she said to Olivia. Then she turned to India. "And you go and get my mum and dad. Go as fast as you can!"

Without a word Olivia and India did as they were told, running off in opposite directions. Jazz had just started scrambling up the bank but she turned and went back down again when she saw Olivia and India running off for help.

Jazz's brother was stretching his arm out towards Tod. "Come on, Tod! Try to get hold of my hand."

Zoe could see that little Tod was never

going to be able to reach Jazz's brother's hand. And suddenly she knew exactly what to do. She plopped herself down on her bottom and started to shuffle down the bank. It wasn't easy and she guessed she must look really clumsy, but she didn't care.

Jazz was looking from Tod to Zoe. She had tears in her eyes. Tod was splashing about in the water and Zoe had the horrible feeling that this might be the only thing that was keeping him up. He wasn't screaming any more. He was crying.

"Can't reach..." he whimpered to Jazz's brother. "It's freezing..."

"Keep on splashing," said Jazz, looking very pale. "The grown-ups are on their way."

Jazz's brother was reaching out as

far as he could, trying to encourage Tod to get a bit closer.

"Can't reach…" said Tod again, in a very small voice.

Zoe saw that she was right next to Jazz's brother now. Quick as a flash she stuck her stick out as far as it would go. "Here, grab this, Tod!" she said in a very firm voice.

Tod looked at the stick with enormous, frightened eyes. "Can't r-r-reach," he stuttered, his teeth chattering with cold.

Zoe knew what she must do. She rolled on to her side and then on to her tummy. Now she could hold the stick out further. The end of it was only just in front of Tod. "Come on, Tod. Grab it!" she said, trying to sound encouraging.

And this time, Tod did.

Chapter Nine

"Good boy," said Zoe. "Now hold tight!"

"Oh my goodness!" came an adult's loud, shocked voice from the path above.

Zoe pulled, but it wasn't making any difference. She didn't have enough strength.

"Can you help me?" she said to Jazz's brother.

But then Zoe got a shock because in a flash, Jazz was lying down beside her, her hand on top of Zoe's hand. They

both gripped the stick together and this time, Tod began to come towards them. As soon as he was close enough to the bank, Jazz's brother grabbed Tod's arm and Zoe pulled the stick towards her. Tod began to whimper softly.

A moment later the woman who had spoken had scrambled down the bank and was crouching beside Zoe. "Come on, sweetheart," she said to Tod, leaning forwards towards him.

He grasped her outstretched arms and the woman pulled him out of the water, then wrapped him tightly in her jacket and cuddled him close. But with one hand she reached for Zoe's hand, and squeezed it. "Thank you so much," she said, in scarcely more than a whisper.

There were more gasps and cries from the top of the bank. And when Zoe

looked round, a whole group of adults had gathered. One or two more of them were making their way down the bank.

"I'm still fr-fr-freezing, Mummy," stuttered Tod, as he snuggled into the jacket.

Jazz had crept into the little space between Tod's mum and Zoe. She suddenly jumped up and called out to one of the grown-ups on the path at the top of the bank, "Mum! Zoe's rescued Tod from drowning!"

Zoe was too amazed to speak. Jazz had helped, after all. And when she looked up, she saw her mum, her dad and Liam among the little crowd up on the path. Jazz's mum was scrambling down the bank.

"Oh my goodness!" she said shakily. "How on earth did it happen, Jade?"

Zoe was puzzled. Why was Jazz's mum calling her Jade?

"Sorry, Mum," said Jazz, her voice cracking. "I told him to come away from the edge, but I was too late. It's all my fault!" And with that she burst into tears.

Zoe felt sorry for Jazz. And Tod's mum must have done too. She put Tod down for a second to give Jazz a quick hug. "Don't be silly, love. It wasn't your fault at all. It's just a good job you've got friends like this!"

Tod's mum was smiling at Zoe.

"I know! Zoe knew exactly what to do, didn't she, Rory?"

Jazz's brother nodded and grinned. Now Zoe felt really puzzled. Jade? Rory? Where had she heard those two names before?

Then Tod suddenly jumped up, and gave Zoe a big hug. "Thank you for getting me out of the freezing cold water," he said, dripping down Zoe's top. "Do you want to hear my rowing song all through now?"

Everyone burst out laughing. And it was at that very moment that Zoe suddenly realised where she'd come across the names Jade and Rory before. Jade was the name of the girl who had written to her about the guinea pigs. And in the letter she'd said she had a brother called Rory.

Could it be? Could it possibly be…?

"Jazz," said Zoe slowly. "Is your real name Jade?"

Jazz nodded. "But at school they call me Jazz," she said.

"Did you write to someone about

some guinea pigs, by any chance?"

"Yes…" said Jazz, sounding surprised. "How did you know that?"

"Because it was *me* you wrote to!" said Zoe.

Jazz gasped. "Why didn't you put your name on the advert?"

Zoe's eyes flew open. "I thought I had done. Why didn't you put your address?"

Jazz clapped her hand to her mouth. "I thought *I* had done!"

Then the girls looked at each other and burst out laughing.

"*Please* can you listen to my song all through now?" Tod asked Zoe and Jazz.

"Just a minute, darling," said his mum. Then she spoke to Zoe. "I can't thank you enough for saving Tod, Zoe. You did some very quick thinking there!"

A lovely warm feeling spread all

through Zoe's body. Then Jazz turned to her mum.

"Zoe's the one who learns keyboard with Mrs Willets, like me," she said.

"I'm so pleased to meet you, Zoe. Jade told me about the piece you composed. She said it sounded brilliant!"

Zoe looked at Jazz, wide-eyed and open-mouthed. And suddenly she couldn't keep quiet a moment longer. "I thought you didn't like me?" she said softly.

"Didn't like you?" said Jazz, looking upset. "Why did you think that?"

"Because...because you never really seem to want to look at me."

"Oh...I thought...I mean, Mum told me that I mustn't ever stare, so I've been trying really hard not to."

Zoe frowned as she thought about

that for a few seconds.

"*Now* can I sing my song all through?" asked Tod, jumping up and down impatiently.

"OK," said Zoe. "Only don't sit so near the edge this time!"

And as everyone burst out laughing, Jazz whispered to Zoe. "I was wondering..." then she suddenly interrupted herself. "No, it's all right."

"What?" asked Zoe.

"You probably won't want to..." said Jazz.

"Won't want to what?" asked Zoe, puzzled.

"Well I was wondering if you could teach me how to compose like you do... I loved that piece you made up so much. I was listening outside the door when you played it at Mrs Willets's. I thought

it sounded like a lake... You didn't mind that I made up the title, did you?"

Zoe shook her head slowly. She couldn't believe what she was hearing.

"Are you sure?" asked Jazz looking anxious.

Zoe suddenly realised she'd been in a daydream, thinking about how different it was going to be at school from now on, because she didn't have anything to worry about now.

"I'd love to help you compose," she said to Jazz.

"Cool!" said Jazz excitedly.

Then both girls broke into big smiles as they joined in the singing...

"...Life is but a dream!"

Look out for...

Make Friends with

Jade

Jade loves being bridesmaid –
but will she like her dress?

Make Friends With

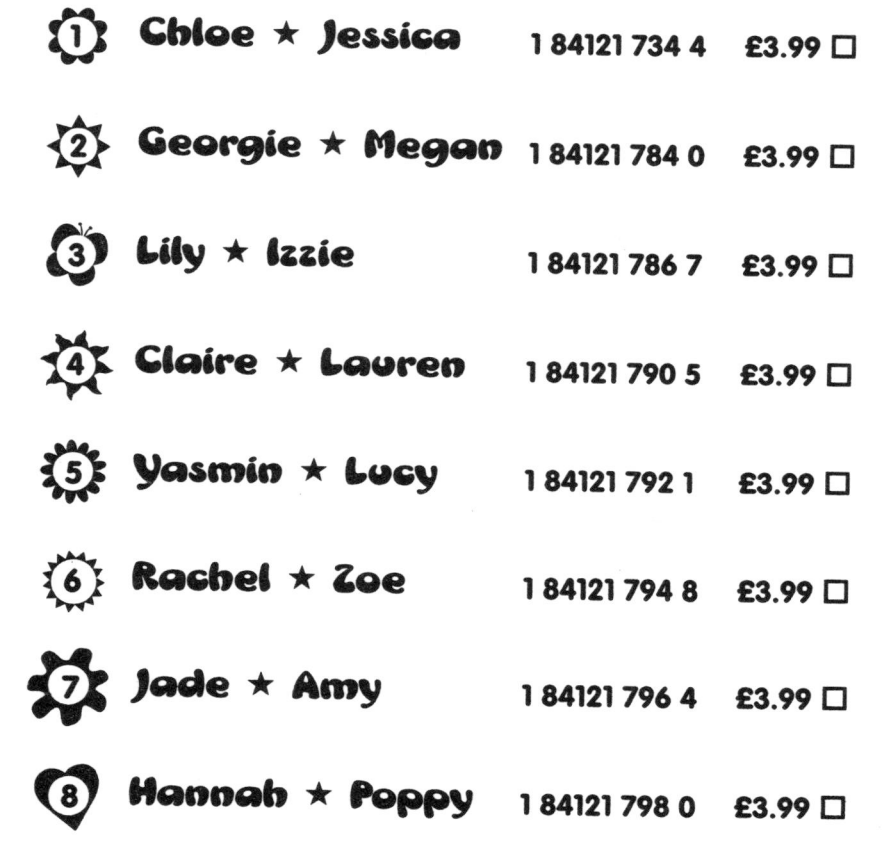

1. **Chloe ★ Jessica**   1 84121 734 4   £3.99 ☐

2. **Georgie ★ Megan**   1 84121 784 0   £3.99 ☐

3. **Lily ★ Izzie**   1 84121 786 7   £3.99 ☐

4. **Claire ★ Lauren**   1 84121 790 5   £3.99 ☐

5. **Yasmin ★ Lucy**   1 84121 792 1   £3.99 ☐

6. **Rachel ★ Zoe**   1 84121 794 8   £3.99 ☐

7. **Jade ★ Amy**   1 84121 796 4   £3.99 ☐

8. **Hannah ★ Poppy**   1 84121 798 0   £3.99 ☐

Who will YOU meet next?

Make Friends With books are available from all good bookshops,
or can be ordered direct from the publisher:
Orchard Books, PO BOX 29, Douglas IM99 1BQ
Credit card orders please telephone 01624 836000
or fax 01624 837033
or e-mail: bookshop@enterprise.net for details.

To order please quote title, author and ISBN
and your full name and address.
Cheques and postal orders should be made payable to
'Bookpost plc.'
Postage and packing is FREE within the UK
(overseas customers should add £1.00 per book).

Prices and availability are subject to change.

Coming up next in...

Make Friends With

Zoe

Zoe's had a brilliant idea –
but will it all work out?

Flip me over!